Growing with Love

Donna E. Buford

Published by Green-Butterfly, 2019.

This is a work of fiction. Similarities to real people, places, or events are entirely coincidental.

GROWING WITH LOVE

First edition. February 14, 2019.

Copyright © 2019 Donna E. Buford.

ISBN: 979-8224815647

Written by Donna E. Buford.

Also by Donna E. Buford

Growing with Love

Watch for more at www.donnaebuford.com.

Table of Contents

First Meeting...

He walked up to stand next to his brother, trying to keep his jaw from dropping. Both were watching three women riding horses. He recognized one as his brother's longtime girlfriend. Of the other two he only remembers seeing the one with dark hair hanging out from time to time. He found himself mesmerized by the redhead riding a horse that he thought wasn't quite broken.

"Ferris, you okay," his sibling asked, looking at his slack-jawed brother.

"What, Fallon," Ferris answered, shaking his head to clear it.

"I asked if you were okay," Fallon said, smiling and shaking his head.

"Oh, yeah, just, who's the redhead," Ferris asked, not breaking his gaze.

"Not sure, I think she's Keara's sister. More of a third wheel if you ask me," Fallon answered.

"Why is she riding that horse? I thought he wasn't fully broken yet," Ferris asked, ignoring the last of his brother's comment.

They continued to watch for a bit longer, when Fallon's girlfriend trotted her horse over. As the horse came up it lowered its head for a scratch from Ferris. He scratched the horse's head, never taking his eyes off the mesmerizing redhead, barely paying attention to the conversation going on.

"Ferris," Fallon said with no response.

"Earth to Ferris," his brother's girlfriend tried.

"Sorry, what did you say, Brighid," Ferris said, still dazed.

"Oh, man you have it bad, bro," Fallon teased his brother.

"What are you talking about, Fallon," Ferris asked, sounding irritated with his brother.

"I mean the redhead you have been staring at since you arrived. Dude, she's a nobody, why are you even staring at her," Fallon chided his brother.

"She is beautiful," Ferris told his brother honestly.

"She's a freaking doormat, Ferris, there is no way you would or could like her," Brighid said with a hint of disgust in her voice.

Ignoring both of them, Ferris turned back to watch the redhead ride the horse that he thought wasn't quite tamed yet. Brighid and Fallon went back to talking, shaking their heads at Ferris. While Ferris was watching, Keara rode over to the fence to join Brighid. Her horse lowered its head for a scratch on the ears from Ferris, which he did.

"Ferris, right," Keara said as she got off the horse she was riding.

"Yes, that's correct. The redhead that's still riding, is she your sister," Ferris asked as he managed to glance at Keara.

"Yes, that's my sister, Kaeley. Why," Keara answered with a smile.

"No reason. Just don't remember seeing her before, that's all," Ferris answered, looking back toward Kaeley.

"She's been here plenty of times, but she mostly hangs out in the barn. I told her she needs to get out and ride today. I'm beginning to think that it was a good thing," Keara said with a sly tone.

"She's a loser, Keara. Definitely not a good match for Ferris at all," Brighid said with disgust in her voice.

"And what? Your sister who is still in her teens would be the perfect match," Keara spit back at Brighid.

Not getting her way, Brighid got off her horse, turned to Fallon, and started talking to him. Keara just shook her head and looked from her sister to Ferris as she scratched her horse's ears. Ferris continued to watch Kaeley ride the horse.

"Keara, is that the horse that they are trying to break," Ferris asked, breaking his gaze to look at Kaeley's sister.

"Yes, it is. Amazing isn't it? She's the only one the horse will let on him without bucking her off. Of course, I think part of it is she doesn't let him get away with it, the other part is she seems to have a natural connection to animals," Keara said with pride.

"Amazing," Ferris said, looking back to the horse and Kaeley.

At that point Kaeley managed to get the horse to change into a trot, then a slow walk, and guided him over to where everyone was standing and chatting. She recognized Fallon, the loud mouth jerk who was Brighid's long-time boyfriend, thinking to herself they were perfect for each other, but she didn't recognize the dirty blond with hazel gray eyes talking to her sister. As she got off the horse and lifted her sunglasses Ferris noticed she had the palest gray eyes he had ever seen. Wow, was the first word to come to his mind and he hoped it wouldn't come out of his mouth.

"Kaeley, this is Ferris. He is Fallon's brother. Ferris, this is my little sister, Kaeley," Keara said, introducing them.

"Nice to meet you," Kaeley said as she nodded her head, not wanting to let go of the horse's reigns for fear of him bolting.

Ferris found himself dumb struck and could only nod his head in response.

"Kaeley, here, take the horses back to the barn and take care of them for me," Brighid ordered as she pushed the reigns from her horse into Kaeley's hands.

"No worries, I got my horse," Keara said as she started to guide the horse she rode back to the barn.

"No, let your loser sister take all of them. She had to tag along anyway, so she gets to do all the grunt work," Brighid said in a very haughty and demanding tone.

Keara sighed and handed the reigns over to her sister. Kaeley just shrugged and half smiled at her sister as she guided the horses back to the barn. Hopping the fence, Ferris glared at Brighid as he ran up beside Kaeley and took hold of a set of reigns from her hand, barely brushing her skin. Both just looked at each other as a small jolt of electricity jumped between them.

"You know you don't have to take that from her, right," Ferris asked, not looking at her but at the ground, only to be sure the words came out in the right order, or at all.

"I know, but she's my sister's best friend and they have enough issues without me adding to it by voicing my feelings," Kaeley responded, looking up at him briefly, "Thanks for helping, by the way."

"Not a problem. It was either help you or tell the bleach blond bitch off," Ferris said with a smile. "I choose to help the damsel in distress."

She just smiled as he said that, and he saw a blush creeping up on her cheeks. He thought to himself that he scored at least one point in his favor. In reality he had actually scored two points, one for calling Brighid a bitch and two for helping her. Kaeley was thinking to herself that things seemed very comfortable around him, a first.

"His stall is at the end on the left. No worries, he'll behave for you," Kaeley said as she guided Ferris to her horse's stall.

Kaeley guided her two horses to their respective stalls and was getting ready to take their bridles off when she heard a commotion at the other end of the barn. When she turned around, she saw that Ferris was having issues with her horse, which wasn't quite tamed yet. Taking a deep breath to steady herself, she locked the stall doors and headed to the end of the barn to calm the wild horse. As soon as the horse saw her, he calmed right down. Ferris turned to see why the horse had a sudden change in temperament and saw her coming toward the stall.

"Sorry about that, he seems to only be calm around me. They can't figure out why," Kaeley said as she neared the stall.

"I think your sister said it best. She told me you seem to have a natural connection to animals," Ferris said, trying to keep calm and hoping silently his words were making sense when they came out of his mouth.

"She's right. For some reason I can get along better with animals than humans any day," Kaeley said as she scratched the horse's head.

"He seems much calmer with you," Ferris said aloud.

"That's because I'm calm with him. It makes a difference in how you approach an animal. You need to be calm and respectful, as they sense the fear and will react accordingly," Kaeley said as she reached for Ferris' hand and placed it on the horse's head, "Here, let me show you. Take a deep calming breath. There, you see? You are calm, and the horse is calm."

"Wow," was all Ferris could get out.

"Come over here, boy, let's get this bridle off you, that should make you feel better," Kaeley said as she reached around the horse's lowered head to release the bridle.

"I can take that back to the tack room for you," Ferris said as he held out his hand for the bridle.

Their hands brushed again, causing the jump of electricity between them and butterflies in both of their stomachs. Ferris took a deep breath as he walked towards the tack room, silently hoping his attraction to Kaeley wasn't showing too much; he knew that a particular part of his body could give him away very easily. While he was trying to slow everything down with deep breaths in the tack room, Kaeley was in the stall with the wild horse, brushing him and talking to him about Ferris.

"Oh, boy, what do I do? He makes me weak in the knees," Kaeley said as she started brushing his mane and continued to muse about the handsome man she just met, "He obviously likes me, I couldn't miss that, but I needed to keep my eyes on you or he would have been very embarrassed, I'm sure."

Hearing the mumbling coming from the horse's stall, Ferris quietly crept out of the tack room and stood next to the stall door to listen while she worked on brushing the horse. Unfortunately, the horse saw him and whinnied with a snort. Hearing the horse's alert, she looked up and saw

Ferris standing outside the stall. Putting the brush on the shelf, she came out, locked the door and just looked at Ferris. The horse just took its nose and pushed gently on her back, making her stumble into Ferris' arms. While they were staring into each other's eyes, Kaeley's sister, Keara, came in and started to unbridle and brush her horse, smiling to herself all the while.

The next thing Kaeley knew, she and Ferris were passionately kissing. He gently tasted her lips with his tongue, thinking she tasted so sweet. Much to his surprise her lips parted, allowing his tongue further into her mouth. While kissing her, he tried to keep his hands at her waist, but they slipped a little down to cup her ass. Kaeley was thinking to herself that she and Ferris seemed to fit in more ways than one. Just as they had to stop for air, they heard the distinctive voice of Brighid crashing in. Kaeley just put her head on Ferris' chest, trying to catch her breath. He instinctively stroked her hair and soothed her.

"You can do this, you can speak your mind. I have a feeling your sister will not mind in the least," Ferris whispered to help her gain her confidence, "Besides, you will have me right behind you cheering you on."

"I just don't know, Ferris. I'm the meek, mild one who wouldn't hurt a fly. I've always blended into the background and..." Kaeley paused her whispering to think about the next portion of her refusal.

"And took the abuse from others taking advantage of your good nature," Ferris whispered as he pulled her head up to face his. All she did was nod and look away, "Well, today is the first step of you standing up for yourself and I will be right behind you to catch, coach, love and help you grow to be the confident woman I see behind those beautiful pale gray eyes."

Did he just say what I think he said? We just met, but it does feel right, we seem to fit. Wow, someone other than my family that loves me for me and he just met me. Deep breath, Kaeley, you can do this. You have him and Keara cheering for you, Kaeley thought to herself.

With a deep breath, Kaeley stepped around Ferris to face Brighid, who was still yelling about something to Fallon. She looked in the other stalls and noticed that Keara was grooming the horse she rode. Just as she was about to say something Keara motioned Kaeley forward toward Brighid. Kaeley nodded, took a deep breath and moved forward even closer to Brighid.

"What did you say," Kaeley asked in the sweetest tone possible.

"I didn't say anything to you, loser," Brighid responded back in a haughty tone.

"I wasn't talking about just now I was talking about when you first came in. I thought I heard my name and Ferris' name," Kaeley said, a little more confident.

"I'm surprised you heard anything with the way you were sucking face over there," Brighid spat at Kaeley.

She was about to turn and walk back to the stall, because she felt the tears welling up behind her eyes and knew that was not good. Then she felt hands on her shoulders and from the electricity jumping she immediately knew it was Ferris behind her, getting ready to catch her just like he said he would. With a deep breath she let all the emotion out. All the anger of years of verbal abuse from Brighid came bursting out in a torrential storm of words. Brighid just stood there with her mouth open in surprise. Keara stood back and smiled as she continued to groom her horse. When Kaeley was done she knew she was about to collapse and just as she felt herself getting weak, Ferris' strong arms wrapped around her, catching her as he had promised.

Three Weeks Later ...

Kaeley was frantically searching through her closet for something to wear and was getting more frustrated by the minute. Keara walked by her sister's room and stopped in the doorway as she saw clothes flying from behind the door onto the bed. Shaking her head, she continued down the hallway. When she heard a loud sigh of frustration coming from the bedroom behind her, she turned around and headed back to see what the issue was. Keara knocked on the door frame before entering into a whirlwind of clothes on the bed, floor, and chair.

"What's wrong, Sis," Keara asked cautiously.

"I'm supposed to have dinner with Ferris and his parents tonight and I have nothing to wear," Kaeley answered with a large sigh as she looked at the bed.

"What do you mean you have nothing to wear," Keara asked, looking around the room with confusion.

"Ferris warned me that his mom is very, very conservative and believes all women must wear dresses below the knee, no slacks, no jeans, and no cleavage showing. All my dresses are above the knee with some cleavage showing. Arg," Kaeley answered as she flopped on her bed and stared at the ceiling.

"Okay, sounds like you need some intervention help here," Keara said as she grabbed her sister's phone and speed dialed Ferris.

"Hello, sweetheart," Ferris answered.

"Sorry, wrong sister," Keara answered with a smile.

"Keara, what's wrong," Ferris asked with a worried tone.

"Kaeley's having a meltdown. I thought you might be the only one who may be able to talk her off the ledge," Keara said in a more serious tone.

"Am I on speaker," Ferris asked before continuing.

"Sure are," Keara said with a smile.

"Kaeley, sweetheart. What's wrong," Ferris asked with loving concern.

"I have nothing to wear," Kaeley said as she grabbed a pillow to hug.

"Sweetheart, I've seen your closet you have plenty to wear."

"Nothing to meet your mom's approval. I want to make a good impression on your parents. I want them to like me."

"Oh, boy. Honey, personally I could care less what my parents think of you. I fell in love with you for you and the strong independent woman I know you can be, not the woman my mom wants me to marry. Trust me, I don't want to marry my mom," Ferris said with a sigh, "Why don't you wear your favorite dress with some leggings? At least your knees will be covered by something."

"Good idea," Keara jumped in, trying to help.

"Keara, think you can take it from here," Ferris asked.

"Yep, sure can, Thanks for the assist," Keara said.

"Welcome. Sweetheart, I'll be there in about a half an hour or so to pick you up," Ferris said.

"Ok. I love you," Kaeley said as she hung up the phone.

Keara pulled Kaeley off the bed and started to sort through her sister's clothes, looking for the dress Ferris was talking about. After finding Kaeley's favorite green dress, Keara moved over to Kaeley's dresser and found a pair of light gray leggings that complemented the dress. After that she dug through Kaeley's shoes and found a pair of light gray flats to complement the outfit.

"There. What do you think, Sis," Keara asked her sister.

"Okay, okay. I like it. Besides, like Ferris said I'm dating him, not his parents," Kaeley said, sounding a little surer of herself.

"Good. I'll leave you to getting ready and will send Ferris back when he shows up. That is if you aren't ready by then," Keara said with a smile as she walked out of the bedroom.

Twenty minutes later Kaeley was half dressed when a knock on the door frame startled her. She turned to see who was at the door. Ferris just stood there looking at her with a big smile on his face. She shook her head as she moved from the mirror over to the bed to put her dress on.

"You sure do know how to scare me," Kaeley said as she pulled the dress over her head.

"I actually debated on knocking at all," Ferris said with a sly smile as he walked into the bed room.

"Good thing you knocked, I would have cussed you out for just standing there not saying a word," Kaeley answered, looking at him with a sparkle in her eyes.

"Wouldn't want you to start the evening off mad at me for scaring you," Ferris answered lovingly as he embraced her in a hug before she could put her arms down to her side.

She looked up into his eyes and all her worries melted away. Smiling, he looked down at her and started kissing her. She tentatively tasted his lips and gently pushed her tongue into his mouth. She melted into him just as she did the first time they kissed. He pulled away first to look at the clock and sighed.

"As much as I'd like to do this all evening, we probably should get going," Ferris said with a sigh of frustration.

"What's for dinner," Kaeley asked as she pulled away and straightened her dress.

"Dad's actually taking us out to dinner. He figured it would accomplish two things. One, give Mom a break from the kitchen and two, in public she'll be on her best behavior, so no scenes will be happening."

"Ah, your dad is one smart man," Kaeley said with a smile as she grabbed her purse and headed out of the bedroom with Ferris right behind her.

Several Hours Later ...

Kaeley was curled up on the bed crying, still in her dress, leggings and shoes. Ferris was out in the living room trying to explain what happened and why Kaeley was crying so hard. Keara was blaming him for her sister crying, not listening to what he was saying. The girls' parents were trying to get Keara to calm down.

"Keara, please go to your room. Yes, I know you are an adult and can do what you want. I am asking you to please remove yourself from this situation and go to your room to cool down," the girls' father asked in an ordering tone.

"But, Dad, he....," Keara started to protest.

"No buts, go now. Besides I have a feeling he had nothing to do with your sister crying," the girls' mother sweetly said.

"I will make you pay for hurting her, Ferris," Keara stormed off down the hall to her bedroom.

"I didn't do anything to hurt her, I hope you know that," Ferris said in a defeated tone.

"We know that, Son. Remember, I know your mom and dad. I am not at all surprised that your mom pulled what she did, even in public. What surprises her Mom and me is that she stood up for herself," Kaeley's father said.

"Ferris, dear, he's right. We both know your parents and are not at all surprised. We are not mad at you or at Kaeley. We actually like how she has been growing, with your help. What we are trying to understand is why she is taking it so hard," Kaeley's mother explained.

"It's only the second time she stood up for herself since I met her. The first time she collapsed, it's a good thing I was behind her to catch her. I think she is so loving and easy going, standing up for herself takes everything out of her. Tonight, I think she is crying because my mom disowned me for taking Kaeley's side of things," Ferris tried to explain his side of the story without Keara there to interrupt him.

"Oh, dear, that would explain it. She feels it's all her fault that your mom disowned you," Kaeley's mom sighed, "Go to her, hug her, hold her. She needs to be reassured everything is okay and I think it should be you."

"I was actually going to ask if I could crash here for the night. I can sleep on the couch," Ferris asked, "Mom told me not to show my face as long as I'm with Kaeley."

"Yes, you can stay. Not a problem. And as for the couch, nonsense. Kaeley's going to need you tonight. Now go to her," Kaeley's father said.

Nodding, Ferris turned and headed down the hall to Kaeley's room. He paused at the door, getting ready to knock, and decided against it. He opened the door and walked in, closing the door behind him. Once inside her bedroom he curled up on the bed behind her and just held her. She melted into him, tears still streaming down her face, but feeling calmer. She closed her eyes and drifted off to sleep. He just laid there holding her as close to him as he could, hoping it would comfort her enough. He hated seeing her in so much pain, and it was because she stood up for herself. Sighing, he ended up drifting off as well.

He woke up, looked at the clock for the time and noticed it was a few hours later. Rolling over onto his back he realized why he was awake, Kaeley was no longer beside him. Stretching, he got up to see where she disappeared to, trying to be as quiet as possible because he didn't want to wake the whole house up. Before he left the room, he looked over at the arm chair to make sure she wasn't sitting in it. Stretching once more, he headed into the hallway. He saw a light coming from the kitchen, so he headed in that direction to see if that's where she disappeared to.

Looking into the kitchen, he saw it was Kaeley. She was sitting at the table eating ice cream.

"Hey, sweetheart, what are you doing," Ferris asked as he walked into the kitchen and sat down at the table across from Kaeley.

"Huh," Kaeley said as she slowly looked up from her ice cream, "Oh, I didn't want to wake you."

"I just woke up. How long have you been up, Honey?"

"Only a minute or so. I was depressed so I came out here to drown my sorrows in some chocolate chunk ice cream."

"Oh, sweetheart. I'm here for you no matter what. I'm choosing you because you are beautiful, strong, loving and independent. My mom's a bitter prude. I will always be here for you no matter what comes our way. Do you hear me," Ferris said as he looked into her eyes with love.

"I hear you. I love you so much, Ferris. I don't know what I'd do without you. I'm just sad that because of me you have lost your mother," Kaeley said, on the verge of tears again.

"Don't even go there, Honey. It was my choice to stand by your side, not yours," Ferris said as he stood up to walk behind her, "Now what do you say we put the ice cream away, go back to your room, get you out of your dress clothes and go back to sleep?"

"Is sleep what you have in mind," Kaeley asked with a sly tone in her voice.

"Only what you want to do, sweetheart," Ferris said in a comforting tone as he guided her back down the hallway to her room.

He led Kaeley into the room. As he shut the door behind him, she turned her night stand light on. Smiling, he reassured her only as far as she wanted to go, if she just wanted to spoon like they did earlier then that's all they would do. She shook her head, pulled her dress off and tossed it to the floor, smiling. Shaking his head, he pulled her into him and started kissing her with the intention of going only as far as she wanted to. He followed her lead, knowing it would give her a little more of the self-confidence she needed. Deep down he hoped she would want to make love but would understand if she didn't.

To his surprise she started taking his shirt off. He followed her lead and started to take off her bra, then let his hands slide down her back to her hips and ass. Kaeley moved her hands down his ribs to his waist, undid his belt and slid his slacks down his hips. Ferris was surprised to not feel Kaeley wearing underwear under her leggings as he slid his hand under the waistband to gently push them down her hips. He pulled away just a little to ask her if she was sure and she pulled him right back in for a deeper kiss. Her tongue gently licked his lips until he opened his mouth for their tongues to dance together.

Next thing he knew, she turned them around and he was lying on her bed with her in complete control. Her leggings were still on, while she was taking his boxers off, exposing his arousal. All she did was look at him with a sly smile. Then she knelt on the bed, bent over him and took the full length of him into her mouth, sucking gently, while moving up and down his length and massaging his balls until he touched her shoulder. He was too close to cumming and wanted to wait for her if at all possible, as he wanted both of them to cum at the same time.

"My turn to pleasure you, sweetheart," Ferris said in a gentle, hoarse whisper.

She moved up on her bed to lay next to him and just smiled. He rolled over onto his side to face her, moving his hand down her stomach, his mouth stopping for a brief moment to suckle one of her breasts and tease her nipple with his tongue while one of his hands moved to the top of her leggings. His other hand was gently massaging the other breast and teasing the other nipple. Once his hand came to the top of her leggings, he rolled over to straddle her legs and started to pull her leggings off, discovering he was right about her missing underwear.

"No underwear," Ferris asked as he raised an eyebrow, smiling.

"Nope," was all that Kaeley answered.

"Wow, you know that move took some self-confidence."

All she did was nod and direct him back to her leggings. He smiled and asked if she was sure about making love that night. She nodded, again, smiling at him with the loving independence he had fallen for three weeks earlier. He quickly finished taking her leggings off and proceeded to tease her by gently caressing her folds between his fingers, then moving inside her folds, he gently probed to find her G-spot. When her back arched he knew he was doing something right. He continued his teasing by moving both hands to her breasts and began alternating between teasing her folds with his tongue and thrusting his tongue inside her.

He moved up and asked her again if she was sure before entering her. Unable to speak, she nodded yes. He slowly entered, stopping briefly to let her adjust to his size as she was very tight, and made love with her. Neither one dominated the other. Finding a slow rhythm that worked for both of them, they looked into each other's eyes and starting kissing deeply as their rhythm quickened the closer each came to climax. At the climax, they came at the same time and continued to kiss during the magical release, so they wouldn't wake anyone up. They both drifted off to sleep while still intertwined looking into each other's eyes.

The next morning...

Ferris was first to wake up to muffled sounds in the other room. He just laid there trying to get his bearings as he woke up in an unfamiliar room. After a second or two he remembered that he was sleeping in Kaeley's room. Smiling, he stretched and rolled over to hold Kaeley, only she wasn't beside him. He sat up and listened closer to the voices drifting down the hallway. Shaking his head, he got up, put his clothes on and headed to the bedroom door. Just as he reached for the door knob the door was flung open, causing him to quickly step back before it hit him in the jaw. He looked to see who was so angry and saw his fiery redhead with gray eyes darker then he'd ever seen them. After slamming the door shut, she let out a loud scream.

"What's wrong, sweetheart? Was it something I did," Ferris asked cautiously.

"No, it's nothing you did, Honey. It's that stupid sister of mine, she's not listening to a thing I'm telling her," Kaeley said after she took a deep breath, "She's blaming you for me hurting last night."

"I'll go talk to her," Ferris said in a very calm voice as he reached for the door knob.

"No don't, honey. Mom and Dad are trying to talk some sense into her. I would just like you to hold me," Kaeley said, trying not to cry.

"Oh, sweetheart, come here," Ferris said, opening his arms to wrap them around her.

"I just...," Kaeley started to say as she put her head on his chest with her arms around him.

"Shh, I know, sweetheart, I know," he said as he guided them over to her bed.

Turning around so his back was to the bed he sat down and pulled her onto his lap. Once she was sitting, he began gently rocking her. After a while he noticed that her breathing had slowed, so he cradled her in his arms and stood up. Turning around, he gently laid her down on the bed, pulled up the covers and kissed her forehead. After he saw her curl back up and drift back off to sleep, he quietly left her bedroom, making sure to shut the door as quietly as possible.

He headed down the hallway with purpose in his step, thinking to himself he is now going to deal with her sister and set the record straight. At the end of the hall he looked up as Kaeley's father held up his hand for him to stop. He paused in the shadows, listening to the conversation.

"Keara, why do you think Ferris is the one who made Kaeley cry," the girls' dad asked.

"Because he is making her stand up for herself. Every time she does, she ends up in tears or passing out," Keara stated.

"So, you would like your sister to continue to be a door mat and take all the verbal abuse people dish out to her," the girls' mom asked seriously as she motioned for Ferris to come into the room.

"While you are thinking on that answer, let me explain what happened," Ferris said, coming into the room, Keara nodded in surprise, "The first time she stood up for herself with Brighid, you were rooting for her as well."

"That's because she deserved it. She always treats Kaeley as her servant, not as my little sister," Keara quickly jumped in.

"Exactly. And I told Kaeley that I would be there to catch her, which I did. I knew within just a few minutes of meeting her that she would pass out. As for last night, Kaeley had taken close to two hours of my mom's verbal abuse. I was on the verge of telling my mom off an hour before Kaeley did. Before you even ask why I didn't, it's because Kaeley asked me not to say anything. She wanted to handle it on her own," Ferris explained while looking at the floor, "You don't know how much pain I was in watching her go through that abuse my mom inflicted on her. I was proud of her when she finally exploded."

"I didn't know," Keara said quietly.

"That's because all you saw were Kaeley's tears and you went into protection mode," the girls' mom said, sitting down next to her oldest daughter, "Your dad and I know Ferris' parents and what his mom is like."

"Thank you for understanding," Ferris said, looking at Kaeley's parents, "I jumped in and stood by Kaeley after she and my mom got into a shouting match. That's when my mom stopped yelling, looked at me and said that as long as I'm with...in her words, 'As long as you are with this heathenistic gold-digging slut you are not my son.' That's when Kaeley started crying harder and ran out of the restaurant. My dad just nodded and motioned me to follow her. I grabbed all of Kaeley's belongings and ran off after her. The rest you know."

"Ferris, we had no idea that your mother went there," the girls' father said as he sat down in the nearest chair in shock.

"I didn't say anything because I told myself on our way over here that it was Kaeley's story to tell, not mine. I'm telling it now because sometime during the night I realized it's our story," Ferris said, looking at all of them.

"Where is Kaeley now," Keara asked cautiously.

"Sleeping. I rocked her back to sleep before coming out here to help explain things," Ferris said, looking Keara in the eye.

"I'm going to go apologize to her," Keara said as she got up and headed down the hallway.

Ferris just sat down, trying to figure out his next move. The girls' parents looked at each other, then at Ferris, with a sigh. Just as they were getting ready to say something to him, there was a knock at the door.

"Ferris, why don't you go check on Kaeley," the girls' father said as he stood up to answer the door.

"Sounds like a good idea, Dear. Maybe the two of you can talk about your next step since you need a place to stay," the girls' mom gently directed Ferris.

"Yeah, maybe you're right. Seems like things work out better when we work together," Ferris said, standing and heading down the hallway to Kaeley's room.

As he got ready to open the door, he heard his dad's voice coming from the living room area, making him pause and listen for just a moment. Keara came out of Kaeley's room and was getting ready to say something when Ferris looked at her and mouthed the words, "My dad." She nodded and started toward the kitchen, then paused, turned around and came back.

"I know you and Kaeley have a lot to talk about. Why don't I go get coffees for both of you? While I'm that direction I can see if I find out what they are talking about and fill both of you in," Keara said with a sly smile.

"Sounds like a good idea. I take my coffee the same way Kaeley does, one cream one sugar," Ferris said.

Ferris stood outside Kaeley's door just long enough for the girls' parents to introduce Keara to his father and for her to excuse herself. He heard his mom's name briefly then went into Kaeley's bedroom. Kaeley was laying on her bed facing away from the door. He could hear her sniffling like she was still crying. He knew all this trying to be strong and stand up for herself was wearing her down, so he just curled up behind her and pulled her into his arms. As he did this, he felt her melt into him and her sniffling slowed.

"Oh, Ferris, what are we going to do? Your mom hates me. You don't have a place to live and can't afford to live on your own yet," Kaeley said through a few more sniffles, "I'm sorry for screwing up your life."

"Stop right there," Ferris said as he gently rolled her over, so she was facing him, "You did not screw up my life. I Love You. I don't care what my mom thinks of my soul-mate, do you hear me?"

Kaeley simply smiled through her tears and nodded.

"Good. Now as for what we are going to do, I know I can't afford a place on my own, but maybe, just maybe if we combine our finances, we can afford a small studio apartment," Ferris said with some hope.

"You mean take our relationship to the next level," Kaeley said, sounding a little less melancholy.

"I thought we did that last night," Ferris said with a twinkle in his eye and a sly tone in voice.

"Well, it seems I have come in with coffee at a very interesting point in the conversation," Keara said. She had pushed the door open with her foot as she was carrying three cups of hot coffee.

Kaeley blushed and buried her face in Ferris' chest. Ferris just looked toward the window, trying to compose himself as well. Keara set the coffees down on the top of one of Kaeley's dressers, then went over and closed the bedroom door to give the three of them a little privacy to talk away from their parents.

"Kaeley, sweetheart, come on, let's sit up. I think Keara has some information for us," Ferris said, gently coxing her into a sitting position.

"I do, but first let me say I'm not even going to ask about that last sentence. Your relationship is your business," Keara said as she smiled at the two of them then she sat down on the desk chair.

"Thank you, Sis," Kaeley said as she tried not to blush again.

"Much appreciated," Ferris said while trying to reorganize his thoughts, "Now what news do you bring us about our parents?"

"Well, I heard them talking about your mom and some of the stuff she was saying to Kaeley. I have to say you took it a lot longer than I would have. She had no right to call you out on your religious beliefs like that, let alone call you a slut and a gold digger. Really, how rude of her," Keara said, clearly fuming herself, "Is the religion thing what the two of you were arguing about the whole time?"

"Most of it anyway. The rest of the time was how I put a spell on Ferris and needed to take it off right then and there. I was pretty composed until that point," Kaeley admitted.

"Composed? Okay, I'll go there, you call shouting composed," Ferris questioned.

"I only shouted because she started shouting at me first and would not listen to reason," Kaeley stated.

"I'll give you that, she was first to start shouting. Now what else did you hear," Ferris responded.

Keara proceeded to tell them what else she overheard their parents talking about while she was getting the coffees. His dad said that as much as he would love Ferris to be able to come home, he wasn't able to talk his wife into letting him back into the house. She only had one condition and he knew there was no way Ferris would agree to it.

"What was the condition," Kaeley asked nervously.

"Exactly what Mom asked," Keara said, taking a deep breath, "From what I heard he had to break up with you and go out with the nice girl she has been trying to get Ferris connected with from her church."

"Hell No! I've told her that more times than I care to remember," Ferris said, trying not to explode at Keara.

"That's what your dad basically said," Keara explained as she got ready to continue.

"Kaeley, sweetheart, to help you understand why I don't like her... she reminds me of Brighid," Ferris said before Keara could continue.

"No explanation is needed, honey," Kaeley said as she leaned into him. "Please continue, Keara."

Keara continued on with the suggestion that Ferris's dad had, which was that since he has a few rental properties he could let Ferris live in one for reduced rent, so that his wife is none the wiser. Kaeley and Ferris just looked at each other, then over to Keara, who had stopped talking once she saw them look at each other.

"What am I missing," Keara asked with concern.

"Well...," they both started to say when they looked at each other and smiled.

"You go ahead and tell, Sweetheart," Ferris said as he gently touched her cheek.

"I don't care which one of you tells me, just please stop with the talking in unison," Keara said, just slightly annoyed.

"The talking in unison actually just started," Kaeley admitted. "And we were just talking about pooling our finances and renting a small studio apartment together."

Keara's mouth dropped open and she was speechless for a few seconds before speaking, "Ferris could you...,"

"Yep, you got it, Keara," Ferris said with a smile, "Why don't I head out and let the parents know what we came up with living arrangement wise?" He stood up from the bed, then bent over and gave Kaeley a long kiss before leaving the room to let the sisters talk in private.

Later that afternoon...

Ferris and Kaeley were in her bedroom working on going over their individual assets and liabilities. First, they tried to put it down on paper, but kept having to redo the numbers, so they turned on her computer and pulled up a spreadsheet program. They plugged everything in and used formulas to calculate how much they would have and need to rent a small apartment. After three tries and a point in the right direction from Keara, they finally had totals to present to their parents.

"According to the numbers we can afford one of my dad's one-bedroom apartments or a studio apartment elsewhere," Ferris said as he sat back and stretched.

"I still can't believe my parents and your dad went for the idea," Kaeley said as she stretched, smiling at Ferris.

"Well, they did, and they gave us an option of which way to go, so that's something."

"True. Personally, I think we should go with the studio apartment to start with, it will give us a little extra cash to save up for a wedding, or even to buy a house someday."

"I love how you think. It will also allow Dad an out with Mom, since he doesn't have any properties with studio apartments," Ferris smiled and leaned in for a deep kiss.

"I'm just glad that my parents are allowing you to stay here while we look," Kaeley said as she pulled away for a quick breath.

"Mm, I think we should hurry as I don't know how much longer we can make love in your room and keep you quiet," Ferris said as he pulled her into him and wrapped his arms around her.

Kaeley just smiled and wrapped her arms around his neck, melting into him as she kissed him this time. His tongue tasted her lips, gently probing for her mouth to open and as it did their tongues danced together. After a minute or so of kissing they stopped to breathe. One of Ferris' hands made its way under her shirt to find she wasn't wearing a bra, and the other went under the waist band of the sweat pants she was wearing to find she was possibly not wearing underwear, either. Both these and the kiss only made things worse for him. Groaning, he met her forehead to forehead and looked into her eyes. She had a sly smile that was creeping up to her eyes. He just took a deep breath and shook his head while trying to readjust his jeans, as they were getting a little too tight at the moment.

"Sweetheart, I think you should go talk to our parents about the numbers," Ferris said in a husky voice, seeing her worried look he added, "You got this, honey, I just don't feel comfortable going out there sporting a hard on."

"Sorry," Kaeley said, taking a deep breath, "I can do this, right? I mean it's only my parents and your dad, right?"

"Don't be sorry, sweetheart," Ferris said, smiling gently and taking her face in his hands so she was looking at him, "Yes, and if you can stand up to my mom you can do this. I will join you out there when it's not so obvious how much I love you."

"Okay. Thank you, Honey," Kaeley said with a smile and turned to the door.

Stopping just outside her bedroom door, Kaeley took a deep breath, telling herself that she had this, her safety is not far away if she needs him. Ferris followed her as far as the doorway and silently urged her forward into the living room with their parents. She moved forward into the living room. As Keara was coming up the hallway from her room, she stopped outside of Kaeley's room and noticed Ferris watching her sister.

"Not going with her," Keara asked, surprising Ferris.

"Wow. You know how to make a person jump," Ferris said before answering her initial question.

"You would have seen me if you hadn't been watching my sister's ass," Keara said, trying not to laugh, "Now are you going out there with her or not?"

"Not currently. Let's just say I'll be more comfortable in a couple of minutes," Ferris said, trying not to sound embarrassed about the fact his girlfriend's sister caught him watching Kaeley's ass.

"Really," Keara said, going from skeptical to understanding as she looked him up and down and noticed the obvious bulge in his jeans, "Oh, gotcha. I'll go to help her with back up in the meantime. Think of your mom. It might help."

"Thanks, Keara. Oh, and do you know," Ferris said, sounding concerned.

"Welcome. And if you are referring to last night, yes, we talked. No worries, they won't find out as long as you can turn your little friend into a Shrinky Dink," Keara answered with a smile and continued into the living room.

Kaeley jumped as she caught movement out of the corner of her eye. When she saw it was her sister she relaxed. She was in the middle of explaining the numbers she and Ferris came up with what they figured out they could afford according to the numbers, along with explaining they even figured in all utilities just in case. Keara sat down beside her sister, put a hand around her shoulder and gave Kaeley a smile of encouragement. Kaeley nodded at her sister.

"We also talked about it and decided to go the route of a studio apartment for a couple of reasons," Kaeley said, after taking a deep breath she sped forward, "One reason is we would be able to put more money into savings for the future, whatever that may be for us. Two, we thought it would reduce the amount of friction between you and Missus Farraday."

"Oh, Kaeley, dear, no need to worry your head about that," Ferris' dad said as he looked over to Kaeley with understanding in his eyes.

"We know, Dad, but Mom is not mad at you right now, she's pissed at me and currently we want to keep it that way," Ferris said coming up behind Kaeley and putting his hands on her shoulders, giving a gentle squeeze while smiling at everyone, "Besides we would like to not only save up for a house but for a wedding as well."

Looks of surprise greeted both of them, as they just smiled at each other. Ferris leaned forward and gave Kaeley a quick upside-down kiss. She smiled up at him and over to their parents. Keara's mouth just dropped open as she looked at the two, trying to piece together what was just said. Everyone was silent for a moment, before they all started talking at the same time. Ferris whistled to get everyone to quiet down so they could explain what he just said.

"Ferris, when did you ask her," Keara asked before their parents could speak up.

"Actually, he didn't. We just knew we were meant to be together forever within the first couple of weeks," Kaeley said as she looked up at Ferris.

"She's right. We just knew. We've been talking about getting married off and on for the last week or so now," Ferris replied, kissing the top of Kaeley's head.

"Okay, you know your mom is not going to like that news," Ferris' father said with a deep sigh.

"We know that, Dad. That's one of the reasons why we would like to keep you out of this apartment search decision," Ferris said with a hint of melancholy in his voice.

"He's right, Mister Farraday. After last night's scene, the less you are involved with some of our decisions the better. I really would hate to be the cause of you having marital issues," Kaeley said as she tried to hold back the emotional tears springing to her eyes.

"Oh, Kaeley, there is no need for you to worry about us. We've hit worse rough patches than this. We got through it then just like we will now. But I can say that I will respect your decision to keep me out of the process," Ferris' dad said as he got up, went over and gave Kaeley a hug.

Kaeley and Keara's parents nodded their agreement to what was said by Ferris' dad. Ferris gently squeezed Kaeley's shoulders and kissed the top of her head again, sensing that she was starting to feel embarrassed with all eyes on her. Seeing this gesture of reassurance from Ferris, Keara gently touched her sister's hand to help calm her.

"Kaeley, dear, we all know you are feeling embarrassed and overwhelmed, but please know we are all in your corner," her mother said, "You are growing into a very beautiful, confident woman. We are all very proud of you. Yes, we agree with what you said about the apartment situation, but your dad and I agree that you shouldn't take others' issues as your own, nor should you feel you caused the issues."

"I know, Mom, it's just...," Kaeley started to say when Ferris jumped in.

"It's that big, beautiful heart of yours getting in the way of your brain. Just one of the many things I love about you, sweetheart," Ferris said as he moved around the couch to kneel in front of her and look into her eyes.

Kaeley simply nodded, trying to hold back the tears that threatened every time she felt relieved. Ferris' dad had managed to sneak out at least a couple days' worth of clothes for his son along with some of his personal hygiene items. Ferris and his dad also made plans for him to stop by the house on the night his mom would be out doing mission work for her church, so he could get the rest of his stuff. The girls' parents offered the extra space in their garage attic for him to store his stuff until the two found a place to live. Nothing was said about the sleeping arrangement, which surprised Ferris, but not Kaeley. She knew her parents had no issues with them sleeping together.

Later that Evening...

Kaeley was in her bedroom making room in her closet and chest of drawers for Ferris. Ferris offered to help out around the house as repayment, since her parents would not accept money for rent. So, he was helping in the kitchen with dishes, then out in the garage attic to make room for the rest of his belongings, which were coming over later in the week. When he was finished, he went to Kaeley's room and found her shuffling stuff around in her closet. Smiling to himself, he came up behind her and wrapped his arms around her waist. While kissing her on her neck, his hands wandered under her shirt, searching for her breasts. As his hands found the prize they were searching for, he started to play with her nipples. Smiling, she stopped what she was doing and leaned back into him with a quiet moan which only encouraged him to continue what he was doing.

"Do you know how hard it's been to keep my hands to myself and from letting my favorite appendage give me away today," Ferris whispered into her ear as he continued to play with her breasts.

"Yes, and I guess it's a good thing I didn't tell you that I decided to go commando today as well," Kaeley responded as she moved her head to one side and her hips closer to him.

"Mm, yes, it is, otherwise I would have been in here or the bathroom all day, because the dick wouldn't be listening to reason at all," Ferris said huskily, trying to keep his breathing even, "I suspected, though, and had to think of my mom all day to keep it from giving me away."

"I'm glad it worked," Kaeley said as she shifted her weight to kick off her shoes, "I would have missed my main cheerleader."

"Mm, really now."

She nodded and moved her hips closer to him, arching her back with a moan. One of his hands slowly made its way down her ribs to the top of her sweat pants. Slowly he moved under her waist band to find she was freshly shaved and very smooth. His breath hitched, and his jeans became even tighter and more uncomfortable. Her movement against him to give his hand better access to her sex was not helping matters either.

"Sweetheart, you are making things very difficult here. You know that, right," Ferris' voice was quieter and huskier as he spoke.

"Really," was all she answered.

"Yes, really. I want to do something about it."

"Why don't you?"

"Two words. Your family."

"Mm, no worries there. Didn't you notice the one thing that was not discussed was the sleeping arrangement?"

"Yes, I thought that odd," Ferris answered as he nuzzled her neck.

"They already know. They are very open minded," Kaeley responded as she turned around in his arms.

She stretched up and gave him a deep kiss before pulling away. Once out of his arms she went over to her computer and pulled up iTunes to select her Imagine Dragons playlist for *Radioactive*. Heading back over to where he stood with his mouth open, she reached up and gently closed it, then went over and closed the closet door. Smiling, he went over to her, put his hands on the bottom of her T-shirt and pulled it over her head to admire her half-naked beauty. She stretched up for another deep kiss. This time he put his arms around her waist, moving them down under the waist band to her ass and gently squeezed. She rewarded him with a moan.

"Let's get you out of these," Ferris said as he started tugging her sweat pants down her hips.

"We both have to work in the morning," Kaeley started to protest.

Not answering her, he simply went over to the clock, checked the time the alarm was set for and turned it on before moving back over to her, taking his T-shirt off in the process.

"There. The alarm is on and it's only eight o'clock," Ferris said as he started suckling her breasts with his hands slowly making their way down her body.

With no other argument she gave in and started to help him out of his jeans, trying to take both his boxers off at the same time. Sensing she was having issues with his jeans and boxers, he broke the kiss and finished undressing. Next thing he knew he was lying on her bed with her on top of him. Smiling, he helped her slide onto his member and enjoyed giving the control over to her, as much as she was comfortable with anyway. While she was riding him slowly, he reached up to tease her breasts, then slowly moved one hand down her body until it was at her freshly shaved sex to gently play with her folds. This threw her into a frenzy, making her want to scream. She laid her head on his chest, after which he rolled them both over to continue the pleasure. Slowly they found that rhythm from the night before. He continued to play with her breasts and every time he saw she was about to scream he kissed her. They slowly made love until they both came several times. They were completely spent and fell sound asleep with their limbs intertwined.

Later that week: Moving day for Ferris...

It was nearing dinner time on Friday evening when everyone who helped to move all of Ferris' belongings collapsed on whatever piece of furniture was available. After a couple of minutes of silence, their parents started talking amongst themselves about dinner. Kaeley was closest and heard pizza delivery mentioned; she listened for a little longer before putting her vote in.

"Pizza sounds good, Mom. I vote for at least one veggie and the brownie desert they have," Kaeley jumped in when she heard a pause in the conversation.

"Kaeley, sweetheart, no one mentioned it, but it does sound good," Ferris said soothingly.

"Actually, we were just talking about treating everyone to some pizza and desert. I think we have earned it. What would everyone like," Ferris' dad said.

"You know I eat most any kind of pizza," Ferris answered.

"I'm with Kaeley, veggie and brownie desert," Keara said.

"Anything with meat for me," Fallon said, following suit.

"Alright then, we'll get the food ordered. In the meantime, could the four of you work in the garage attic," the girls' mom responded, "One of us will be out to let you know when the food is here."

"Sure. And that's 'parent' for, 'Get lost. We want to talk amongst ourselves,'" Kaeley and Ferris said together as they stood up.

Kaeley, Ferris, Keara and Fallon all went to the garage attic and looked around. It only took the four of them about ten minutes to move what little bit Ferris had over to one area, all pushed neatly together. They decided to sit down wherever they could find room and talk until their parents came to get them for dinner. Keara and Kaeley decided to talk between themselves as they hadn't had much of a chance all week. While they were talking, Fallon took the opportunity to get caught up with Ferris.

"Okay, little brother answer me this, I noticed we put your clothes in Kaeley's room. Are you already sleeping together," Fallon asked curiously, wanting all the dirty details.

"So what if we are? You jealous Brighid isn't giving you any love since Kaeley and I are dating? Or is it since her father hired her to help train that wild horse of theirs," Ferris shot back to his brother.

"Ouch, low blow, bro, but I deserved it," Fallon admitted.

"Seriously, how are things going with the two of you," Ferris asked.

"Rocky, currently. And for the record, I'm not jealous. I'm happy for you both," Fallon answered, "I was wondering how long it would take for Mom to kick you out as well."

"I think what pushed Mom over the edge is the religion subject. Kaeley and her family are very open minded about other beliefs, and she is a practicing Natural Witch. Mom found out last Saturday at dinner and I stood by Kaeley. You can guess what happened after that," Ferris said, trying not to sound too melancholy.

"Wish I could have seen those fireworks," Fallon said with a laugh.

"What Mom doesn't realize is she just pushed us into the next level of our relationship quicker than we would have gotten there," Ferris said as he looked over to Kaeley and her sister.

The conversations continued for another ten minutes or so before the girls' dad came to get them for dinner. While eating, Fallon chanced to ask what their parents were talking about while they slaved away in the garage attic. All three parents just looked at each other and did not say a word. Ferris slugged Fallon in the shoulder for even asking.

"What was that for, bro," Fallon asked while rubbing his shoulder.

"For even asking. If they wanted us to know we would have been invited to stay while they talked," Kaeley spoke up before Ferris could.

"Oh, now she's your mouth piece, baby bro," Fallon snipped at both of them.

"Kaeley, sweetheart, let me handle this one," Ferris said as he put a hand on Kaeley's knee and stared his brother down, "Fallon, if you can't be polite to Kaeley when she simply speaks what I'm thinking then you can either keep your opinion to yourself or leave."

"How about we take this outside, so you can show me that you have balls? Unless you gave them to Kaeley to hold," Fallon pushed as he stood up.

"He just did not go there, did he," Keara whispered to Kaeley.

"I think he did," Kaeley said, about ready to jump to Ferris' defense.

"Boys. Enough. Fallon, just because your brother has met his soul-mate is no cause for you to think he is whipped. Now you can hold your tongue or leave if you cannot be a civil guest in the Kerr house," the boys' father spoke up, not willing to take any of the nonsense.

"But, Dad ...," Fallon started to whine.

"No buts. I'm taking enough shit from your mom right now, I don't need to take it from you as well. With that said, make your decision now," the boys' father told Fallon sternly.

"Sorry, I didn't mean to be rude," Fallon said sheepishly as he took another bite of pizza.

The rest of dinner was spent in silence. Ferris offered to do the clean-up and Keara said she would help him. Their parents smiled and nodded as they headed outside to the back yard to talk some more. Kaeley kissed Ferris and told him she would be in the bedroom putting his clothes away. Giving her a kiss, he asked if she was sure and okay. She answered with a, sure, and out she went toward her room. Fallon just sat and watched the interaction before getting up and following her. Keara, hearing the chair move, looked over her shoulder to see him following Kaeley.

"What's your brother's deal," Keara took the opportunity to ask Ferris.

"Oh, I think he's a little jealous of Kaeley and I, because his relationship with Brighid is currently on the rocks," Ferris answered as he looked over his shoulder, slightly worried.

Keara, sensing his worry, placed a hand on his shoulder and said, "You know she can handle herself now, thanks to you, right?"

"I know, Keara. I just like to be a little closer to her when she needs a safety net," Ferris said, still sounding worried.

"I've seen her at work recently, and Brighid tried to give her a hard time. All Kaeley had to do was look at her and she backed off. I don't think she needs a safety net that much anymore," Keara said, trying to reassure Ferris.

"Good to know," Ferris said, sounding better, "When I first saw her on that unbroken horse, I knew there was a strong, confident woman in there. I just didn't know how deep it was buried."

Keara just smiled and patted his shoulder in reassurance. They continued to work on the dinner clean-up, putting away what little was left over. When they were done their parents motioned them outside. Looking around they asked where Fallon and Kaeley were. Keara explained that Kaeley was working in her bedroom and Fallon followed. Ferris' dad, looking concerned, excused himself and went inside to check on things, thinking his youngest son may be too trusting of his big brother.

"Fallon, what are you talking about? I can't teach you anything," Kaeley said, sounding confused.

"I know you put a love spell on my brother. I just want the same thing done so Brighid will love me again," Fallon said, sounding desperate.

"Oh, Fallon, take a seat and let me explain this to you one more time, and I need you to pay very close attention," Kaeley said sternly.

Fallon took a seat in her computer chair and she sat on the bed. As she sat, she caught a glimpse of his dad hovering outside her bedroom door, listening. She took a deep breath and asked Fallon to look at her and focus on what she was saying. He simply nodded.

"First, I need you to be honest with me about your relationship with Brighid," Kaeley said empathetically.

"Honesty? You know that's hard, right," Fallon said.

"I know, but for me to properly help you, I need the truth and nothing less," Kaeley responded with understanding.

"Okay. You know that we've been going out for just over a year, right," Fallon said and continued as Kaeley nodded, "Well, I approached her about moving in with me the day you and Ferris met. I wanted to move our relationship to the next level as it almost seemed like we were stuck in the friends with benefits stage. She didn't want to move in with me, so I asked her why not."

"Let me guess. She never answered, right," Kaeley jumped in quickly.

"Yep. You got it. So, she paused things without any reasoning," Fallon answered as he put his head in his hands.

"Okay, Fallon, I need you look at me when I say this, because I'm not going to repeat myself and you didn't hear it from me, either. Do you understand," Kaeley said, sounding suddenly serious.

"Yes. What's up," Fallon said.

"I've told her with her father in hearing distance that she needs to tell you this herself. Evidently, she's not taking my advice," Kaeley said, shaking her head, "She has actually been cheating on you. I saw her with someone else and they were doing more than kissing when I spotted them."

"She's with another guy," Fallon said, sounding angry.

"Fallon, you assume too much. I said pay attention. She was with someone else, I never said if that person was male or female, did I," Kaeley repeated part of what she knew, "My advice to you, is to get her some of her favorite flowers and tell her you want to talk to find out exactly what she wants out of the relationship. Be open minded, listen and take her feelings into account. Tell her your feelings; how you have felt the last few weeks. I think she is confused as well at this point, and she just needs someone who will be there for her no matter what."

"Really? You think that's all she needs," Fallon asked with some hope.

"Not eavesdropping, but if I'm getting the gist of what you just said about Brighid, I can tell you her family does not understand or support her at all," Fallon's dad said as he came in and put his hand on Kaeley's shoulder.

"I'll leave the two of you to talk about this a little more," Kaeley said, smiling as she got up and walked out.

"Thanks for getting the ball rolling, Kaeley," the boys' dad said smiling up at her, "Ferris is outside."

"You're welcome and thanks," Kaeley said as she headed out of the bedroom.

Later that Evening...

Ferris walked into Kaeley's bedroom to see her lying on her stomach with her head at the foot of her bed and her feet at her pillows. She was flipping through her last issue of *Cosmopolitan* and already in her pajamas. Smiling, he joined her, wrapped the arm closest to her around her waist and nuzzled her neck. Exhausted from a full day of lifting, toting and moving, she leaned into him with a yawn. He pulled the magazine out of her hands, got up and placed it on her desk, open and upside down to mark her place, then went back over and coaxed her to flip over so her head was on her pillows. Once she had her head on her pillows, he covered her up. She drifted off to sleep as soon as her head landed on her pillow. As he was getting ready to strip down to his boxers, turn her ceiling fan on and light off, there was a knock at the door.

"Yes," he said as quietly as possible, so he didn't wake her.

"Just making sure everything is okay in here," Kaeley's mom said, cracking the door open.

"Yes. She is exhausted. I just covered her up and was getting ready for sleep myself. Did you need anything," Ferris said as he made his way to the door.

"No, just wanted to check on her. You both had a very busy day."

"She'll be fine. I know you're worried after what happened with my idiot brother, but she handled it like a trooper. She didn't seem as drained as normal this time."

"That's good. I'm glad you found each other, Ferris. I've seen both of you grow over the last four weeks or so. Sleep well, both of you," she said as she started to close the door.

"We will. Thank you," Ferris said as he turned and placed his back against the door.

With a quick flick he locked her bedroom door, just in case. Then he slipped out of his jeans, turned her ceiling fan on and light off before curling up in bed with Kaeley. He put his arm around her from behind and pulled her into his body, to which she naturally formed herself. He drifted off into a deep sleep. Next thing he knew it was three in the morning and someone was rattling the door knob and knocking frantically. Looking next to him, he saw Kaeley groggily sit up as the noise woke her up as well.

"I got it, sweetheart," Ferris said as he stood up, yawning and unlocking the door, "What's going on?"

"Ferris, there's a phone call for you," Kaeley's dad said, sounding frantic. "Why was the door locked?"

"Sorry about that, Mister Kerr. It's a habit I got into during puberty. I learned quickly from watching Fallon go through the Bible lectures against masturbation," Ferris said, slightly embarrassed.

"Ah, enough said. It's your dad, something about Fallon," Mister Kerr answered with understanding.

"Oh, boy. I wonder what that block head brother of mine did now," Ferris said, heading out to pick up the phone in the living room.

"Hey, Dad, what's up with Fallon? Is everything okay," Ferris said as he yawned.

"He's missing! I've called his apartment, no answer, his cell phone, no answer. I went to his apartment, he's not there," Ferris' dad said, sounding frantic.

"Have you tried Brighid," Ferris yawned.

"I tried her dad. He said he hasn't seen her for some time as well," Ferris' dad said hurriedly.

"Hold on a sec, Dad, let me check on something," Ferris said, putting the phone down and going into Kaeley's room, "Kaeley, sweetheart, do you happen to know the name of Brighid's girlfriend?"

"Yeah, it's Anne. Why," Kaeley groggily answered as she rolled over.

"Fallon and Brighid are missing. I thought they might be over there. Do you have her number in your phone," Ferris said, trying to get her to stay awake just a little longer for the answer.

"Yes, it's the only Anne in my contacts. You might want to call her, though, tell her you're my boyfr...," Kaeley said as she drifted back off.

Kissing her on the top of her head, he grabbed her phone. Looking through the contacts, he found Anne's number and tapped it to dial. While it was ringing, he went back into the living room next to the phone with his dad on the line.

"Hello, is this Anne," Ferris asked when the phone was picked up.

"Yes, who's askin'," Anne answered gruffly.

"I'm Ferris, Kaeley's boyfriend and Fallon's brother. Would he and Brighid be over there by any chance," Ferris said quickly.

"Yes, they are. And for the record I told them both to answer their phones when their dads rang through," Anne said with understanding.

"Thanks. Sorry about bothering you so late," Ferris said as he got ready to hang up, "Oh, I'll pass the message along."

"Not a problem, Ferris. Good night, man," Anne said then hung up.

"Dad, I found them. They are at Brighid's girlfriend's place," Ferris reassured his dad as he picked up the phone.

"Thanks, Ferris. How did you find out where she was," his dad answered, sounding relieved.

"Kaeley knew Brighid's girlfriends name and happened to have her as a contact," Ferris answered honestly.

"Okay, I'll let Brighid's dad know they are both at a mutual friend's for the night. Good night, Son," Ferris' dad said as he hung up.

Ferris sighed as he hung up the phone and turned to head back to Kaeley's room, yawning as he walked back in. After closing her door, he went back over and curled up next to her. She was facing him, but he still wrapped his arm around her and gave her a quick kiss. Blinking, she mumbled a question about Fallon. He told her Fallon was at Anne's with Brighid, both of whom were avoiding their parents' phone calls. She mumbled something sounding like good, before drifting back off to sleep. Smiling, he closed his eyes and drifted back into his own deep sleep.

Next Morning ...

Ferris woke up on his back, staring at the ceiling fan spinning and feeling light touches on his stomach and legs. He moaned as he stretched and woke up the rest of his body. Kaeley looked up from what she was doing, moved up and kissed him on the lips. Her hands were searching his body from his chest down to the part of his body that had woken him up. Smiling and closing his eyes, he just let her explore his body and kiss him all she wanted. Next thing he knew she was under the covers sucking on his dick, slowly moving up and down with the gentlest of pressure. Taking a deep breath in surprise, he grabbed the covers as she started to massage his balls, bringing him closer to coming.

"Oh, sweetheart, if you don't stop soon, I'm so close," Ferris said as he reached over and touched her shoulder.

Hearing this, Kaeley increased her pace and looked up at him with mischief in her eyes. With a groan, he put his head back on the pillow to enjoy the morning surprise. Not wanting her family to her, he grabbed her pillow and placed it over his mouth as he screamed when he came hard. She finished him off and swallowed, which surprised the hell out of him. He reached down, touched her shoulder and brought her into his arms to hold her so, as they both briefly drifted back off.

"That was a nice surprise, sweetheart. I'd like to repay the favor," Ferris said when he woke up and gently stroked her face.

"Mm, that would be nice, but...," Kaeley said with a smile.

"Enough said. I'm not going to argue with nature. Besides it's a good thing, right," Ferris said with understanding.

"Yes, it is. We also have a big day of looking at apartments today anyway," Kaeley said in a melancholy tone as she rolled over.

"No, you are not going anywhere yet till you tell me what's wrong," he said as he rolled her back over to look him in the eye.

"Nothing."

"Bull, something's wrong. I can tell. Now what's wrong?"

"Really? Well I guess it's that we have been making love this last week with no protection for either of us," she answered.

"That's bad on my part. I never thought of it. I'm so sorry. We can buy a box of condoms while we are out looking at apartments and other errands," he said, sitting up and taking her in his arms.

"You know how to make me smile. I should have thought of making an appointment for myself, but I really don't want to take chemicals and...," she rambled.

"Shh, no worries, I got this one for us. It'll be a bit uncomfortable but it's better than some of the side effects from the chemical bullshit out there for you," Ferris interrupted, putting both his hands on her cheeks. "Now let's get ready for the busy day ahead, okay?"

Nodding, she smiled, leaned over and gave him a quick kiss before getting up to get dressed. He smiled and stretched once more before getting out of bed himself to get ready. Once they were both dressed, they went to the kitchen to grab some breakfast before heading out to look at the couple of studio apartments and the one-bedroom apartment in their price range. Thankfully, since they were confident that they could make monthly rent and utilities, their parents offered to pay for the security deposit on whichever apartment they chose.

Later that Day around Dinner time...

Ferris and Kaeley decided to go out to eat for dinner to discuss the apartments they looked at earlier in the day. Out of the three they looked at, only two would even let them rent in the complexes; the other one had religious and marital issues, which really steamed Kaeley. It took all Ferris had to keep her from exploding on the manager. Fortunately, that was the last apartment they had to look at that day. Of the other two, only one of them was in a fairly decent area while the other was in a bad part of town, so they nixed that one immediately. They continued talking about the one option left while at dinner.

"I don't know, Ferris, Honey. I'd really like to continue looking for a bit. Don't get me wrong, the one good apartment was nice. Unfortunately, the one I really liked was the one...," Kaeley said in between bites of her pizza.

"I know, sweetheart. I agree, we don't have to rush at least. I was thinking we could do some research on the one that wouldn't let us rent to see if it was just that manager or if it is the whole company's view," Ferris said while she paused to eat.

"True."

"I have a feeling it might be just that manager, but some research won't hurt," Ferris said reassuringly, "Smile, sweetheart, it's only the first week we looked. We'll find the perfect place to start out eventually."

Smiling, she nodded, "I know, it just stings a little, what the last apartment manager said to us," and took another bite of veggie pizza.

"At least it only stings now. If I'm correct, four weeks ago it would have hurt like hell. Right?"

"You're right," she said with a blush.

"Let's finish up here, stop at the store for our list of items and go home to curl up with a good movie. What do you say?"

"I say that's a good idea. I need to get some of my feminine napkins, while you are looking for the condoms."

"I say we get both together, besides they are for both of us, aren't they?"

"How do you figure that?"

"Well, the condoms are so that you won't get pregnant, but you will be feeling the texture. And the feminine pads you need are a good thing, that tells us the protection I'm using is working, that and if I know what kind you use, it will help me in case you need me to pick them up in an emergency."

"Wow. You are simply amazing. Okay, it makes sense. Would you mind if we added chocolate ice cream and chocolate sauce?"

"Not at all," he responded with a smile.

They finished dinner, boxed up the leftovers to go and payed the bill, then left for the nearest big box store to do their shopping. Once in the store they agreed to get the ice cream last, so it wouldn't melt. They picked out a variety pack of Trojans together, then he observed as she picked up a couple packs of her feminine napkins and made mental note of the kinds she grabbed. Finally, they headed over to the frozen food section of the store to pick out the ice cream.

"What kind would you like, Ferris, honey," she asked, looking at the selection in the freezer.

"When it comes to ice cream, sweetheart, I'm not picky at all. So, whatever you would like."

"Okay then how about triple chocolate chunk?"

"Wow, *Death by Chocolate*, sounds sweet and good. Go for it. Why don't you go to the next aisle over and pick out some toppings? I want to grab something else to go with the ice cream. I'll meet you there in a minute or two."

"Sounds good," she said, stretching up to kiss him.

Kaeley found the aisle with the peanuts and other ice cream toppings. She grabbed a jar of peanuts, chocolate syrup, and candy sprinkles. Meanwhile Ferris went looking for the canned whipped cream. When he found it, he picked up two cans and headed back to where Kaeley was, still debating if she wanted any additional toppings. She heard the distinctive clink of metal cans being placed in the cart and turned around to see Ferris with a sly smile on his face and two cans of whipped topping in the cart.

"Hey, Honey. You realize we will have to put our names on those, right," Kaeley simply stated with a wicked smile.

"I'm not even going to ask, just say T D M F I," Ferris responded with a shake of his head as if trying to clear the mental image.

"All that's left is to pick out something to watch," Kaeley said as they started to head towards the check-out counters.

"I was thinking about that. Do you have a Netflix account?"

"No, why?"

"Well, I do, and I found this cool show called Sense8 we can binge watch. I really think you'll love it."

"Sounds good. What's the plot and who directs it?"

"Well, it's written and directed by the Wachowski's. It's about 8 people who...," Ferris started to tell Kaeley when she stopped him.

"You had me at the Wachowski's. Sounds excellent. We can set it up on my computer, if you want."

"No worries, I'll bring my smart Blu-ray player in and connect it to your T.V., if you don't mind getting the ice cream ready while I do that."

"Not a problem."

Back at Kaeley's Home...

Once home, Kaeley took the cold items right to the kitchen. Ferris offered to take the other bag right to her room. He then headed out to the garage attic for his Blu-Ray player to connect to her T.V. for their Netflix binge marathon of Sense8. The only thing they forgot to pick up was bananas; they both figured they had enough toppings anyway. When Kaeley was done making the sundaes she put their initials on all the items and put them away before heading to her bedroom. Carrying both bowls, she was headed down the hallway when her mom saw her and stopped her briefly.

"Hey, dear. Everything okay," her mom asked.

"Yeah, just had an issue with one of the apartment managers we met today. No big deal, nothing I can't handle, now, anyway," Kaeley responded to her mother, holding up the sundaes, "If you don't mind, Mom, we were going to eat our sundaes and binge watch a show on Netflix that Ferris likes."

"Sure, you know that's not a problem. The two of you will fill me in tomorrow though, right?"

"Yep, sure will."

"Here is your sundae, honey," Kaeley said as she entered her bedroom, "Were you able to get everything set up?"

"Thank you, and just finishing up now," Ferris answered as he put in his password.

Setting the sundaes down on her nightstands, she then proceeded to prop the pillows up against the headboard, so they would have a cushion for their backs while they stretched out to eat and watch. Once he finished the set-up, he joined his beautiful, strong, intelligent girlfriend and started up the show. Slowly eating their desert and watching Sense8, they only paused a few times for bathroom breaks, and while on one of the breaks Ferris offered to take the dishes out to the kitchen. When they came to an orgy scene in episode 6, 'Demons,' Kaeley grabbed the remote, pushed the pause button, got up and made sure the bedroom door was shut and locked. Next thing Ferris knew, Kaeley was unzipping his jeans and freeing his favorite body part. She teased the end of his dick with her tongue then took all of him into her mouth. After several minutes of teasing his dick and massaging his balls he warned her he was going to cum, which made her pick up the pace until he exploded in her mouth. Once he was done, she swallowed, then followed with a quick drink of water and kissed him deeply.

"Thank you," was all he said very hoarsely.

"You are very welcome, honey," she said with a sly smile as she settled down back into position to continue the marathon.

"I'm not even going to ask. I'll just accept it," he said as he wrapped his arm around her, pulled her into him and hit the play button.

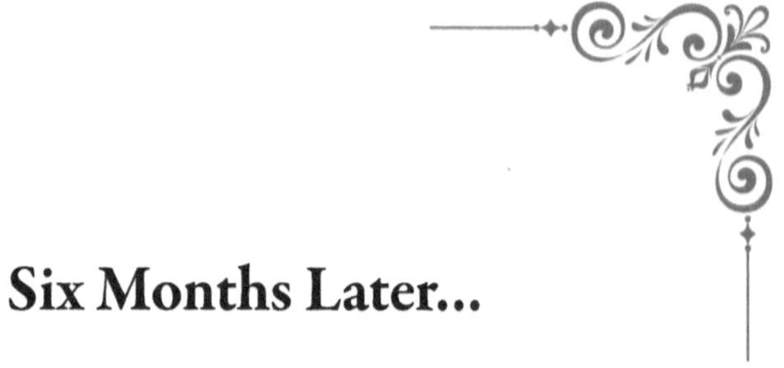

Six Months Later...

Kaeley and Ferris were at her parent's house grabbing the last of the boxes to take back to their apartment. As he was taking the last box to the car, she stepped back inside to talk to her parents and sister because she had only been able to see them once or twice a week over the last three months. Ferris understood that after over twenty plus years, she missed her family and gave her time to visit; heck, most of the time it meant a free dinner.

"I think that's all of it. Now all we have left is to finish unpacking," Ferris said as he came back into the house.

"You both know that you didn't have to hurry and find a place," Kaeley's dad said as he looked in Ferris' direction.

"We know, Dad, but we wanted to at least start our life together on our own sometime before the wedding," Kaeley said as she wrapped her arm around Ferris' waist.

"We know, honey. I can't believe the wedding is only a few months away either," Kaeley's mom said, "Are you two sure you're not moving too fast now?"

"Like you and Dad didn't," Kaeley asked with a tilt of her head.

Knowing their daughter had a point, they both looked at each other and nodded, since the two of them had eloped just a few months after they met. At least Kaeley and Ferris were waiting a year or so to marry. Smiling, her parents looked at their daughter with pride in their eyes.

"What are you two thinking," Ferris asked, seeing their look.

"Oh, just how much Kaeley has grown since meeting you, Ferris," her dad said.

"She has become a very Strong, Beautiful and Independent woman, hasn't she," Ferris said as he leaned down to kiss her.

"I have turned into a Beautiful Butterfly, haven't I," Kaeley said with a smile, "Now I hate to call it short, but we need to get dinner then go to my dress fitting."

"Ugh! That means I need to visit my parents," Ferris said with some melancholy.

"Don't be so down, I'll be there with you. Remember tux fittings for the men, too," Kaeley's dad said as he patted Ferris' shoulder.

The five of them piled into two cars and headed off for a quick dinner together before leaving for the tux and dress fitting appointments. Fortunately for Kaeley, Ferris' mom would be at the tux fitting as she did not want to be in the same room as Kaeley. Kaeley, Keara, Brighid and Kaeley and Keara's mother; for the dress fitting.

"Where's Fallon and Ferris' mom," Brighid asked out of curiosity.

"She said something about not wanting to be in the same room as the heathenistic witch my baby is marrying," Kaeley said with a smile, "I said, 'Thank you,' and promptly told her she would have to be in the same room with me at the wedding as well as have to play nice for several hours. I walked away before I could hear or see her reaction."

"Wow, Sis! Who would have thought that would come out of your mouth," Keara said as she turned to help Kaeley zip up her wedding dress.

"You really have come along way, Kaeley. Also, thanks for the support. You don't know what it means," Brighid said, trying to zip her dress when Keara turned around to help her out.

"Brighid, I do know what it means, and I'm marrying the one who started my self-confidence ball rolling," Kaeley said as she turned to look at herself in the mirror, "Oh, how are things going with the three of you anyway?"

"Still trying to find our way in this very new relationship. Thinking I may end up having the same type of relationship with the brothers' mom as you do, though," Brighid answered with a partial smile.

The three linked arms as they looked at themselves in the full-length mirrors. Kaeley knew she had come a long way in her growing, but knew she had a long way to go. She simply smiled, put her head on her sister's shoulder and pulled both women into her for a group hug. With a supportive sister, best friend and a wonderful soon-to-be husband, she was going to be just fine. She had plenty of good people to help pick her up, dust her off and push her forward again.

Coming Soon: Watch for a full-length book for more about Kaeley and Ferris:

Kaeley has come a long way in the past year but something, or someone, made her bury the self-confidence of her youth. Will Ferris be enough to help her face her haunting past or will he need the help of an old friend? Will Kaeley ever really escape her past or is it better to face it head on before the memories and voice of her mother-in-law win?

PLEASE REMEMBER TO leave a review: (https://books2read.com/u/bzLPq2)

and you can contact me directly with feedback of any type at donna@donnaebuford.com

FOLLOW DONNA:
Facebook: DonnaEBuford[1]
Twitter: DonnaEBuford1[2]
YouTube: Donna E Buford[3]

---

1.   https://www.facebook.com/DonnaEBuford

2.   https://twitter.com/DonnaEBuford1

3.   https://www.youtube.com/channel/UCebMJN3I2HfaC579AOrDy2w?view_as=public

About the Author

Donna has been writing for over 30 years. Her first love is creative writing in all types of fiction and primarily focuses on the self-empowerment of her main characters. She feels her writing is a way for her voice to be heard and to help people ask for the help or support they need to take their first steps toward their own self-empowerment.

Donna lives in Toledo, OH with her family and a library of over 500 books. She also writes children's books, under the name of H.A. Bryan, that focus on self-empowerment while speaking publicly to overcome bullying.

Read more at www.donnaebuford.com.

About the Publisher

Green-Butterfly is the marriage of publishing and Internet marketing. Heather loves writing and has been in the publishing industry since the late 1980's. Cory eats, sleeps and breaths Internet research and marketing. In 2020 the pandemic forced many people out of work and online, unable to earn money and no idea where to begin so Heather and Cory hatched Green-Butterfly.

Green-Butterfly is not a traditional publisher. New authors are welcome to benefit from marketing advice and publishing services are offered on an ad-hoc basis. Those already self-publishing can learn how to work smarter instead of harder. Traditionally published authors can increase their visibility and build credibility while authors not satisfied with their traditional publishers can regain more control over their business.

Read more at https://green-butterfly.org.

* 9 7 9 8 2 2 4 8 1 5 6 4 7 *